Will Ferdinand Find a Friend?

Written and Illustrated
by Debbie Appelman

Will Ferdinand Find a Friend?

Copyright 2016 by Debbie Appelman

First Edition 2016
ISBN 978-0-9976105-8-1

Published by Scorpio Press www.Scorpio.Press

For bulk orders contact Debbie here:

uglydogcreations@gmail.com

I dedicate this book to my
husband who encouraged
me to follow my dreams.

I encourage everyone to
find your cheerleader
because they can help
you tackle the challenging
tasks with their support.

A Message from the Author

for the parents, grandparents, teachers, guardians, mentors

and any other advocate for children.

This book is for all of the people who have felt "invisible" at some time or another. I want you to know you are not alone. I know this, because I have been an "invisible" person in different parts of my life. I also know, although you may appear invisible, you aren't. You want to be included and be part of something larger than yourself. You have permission to join in. Put yourself out there, you will be amazed the wonderful people and adventures you will find.

I also write this book to help children understand the importance of acceptance. As we walk through life, we will encounter people like us and people that are different from ourselves. No matter what we look like, think like, or act like, we are all the same. At our basic needs we are no different---we are human. If we teach our children to accept people for what they have to offer and not how they could change them, then we would live in a wonderful world truly.

I was an elementary school teacher for 16 years working in the public school system. I also have two children of my own that have since gone on to college and work. Reading was a priority in my family and both my children developed the love of books. I write this book as a parent, a teacher and as someone who loves to share books with others. I felt it was important to share a meaningful message in my story for children and to incorporate resources for parents and teachers to help extend learning of the book.

Ultimately, I extend the message, "To treat others with the respect that we would want for ourselves, would make a happy school yard indeed."

Welcome! I am so glad that you opened my book. My name is Ferdinand and I am a lawn ornament.

Wait...don't put this book down! I have an interesting story to tell you about how I became who I am today.

As the morning began, all of the woodland animals visited the area near the bird bath. The yard was very overgrown because a family did not live there.

No one even knew Ferdinand was in the yard
because he was hidden by weeds and
branches. Each day was the same. Ferdinand
watched the birds, squirrels and other woodland
animals playing in the yard, never paying any
attention to him. Ferdinand wanted to be part of
the group but he was hidden from all of the
animals. It was as if he was invisible to
everyone.

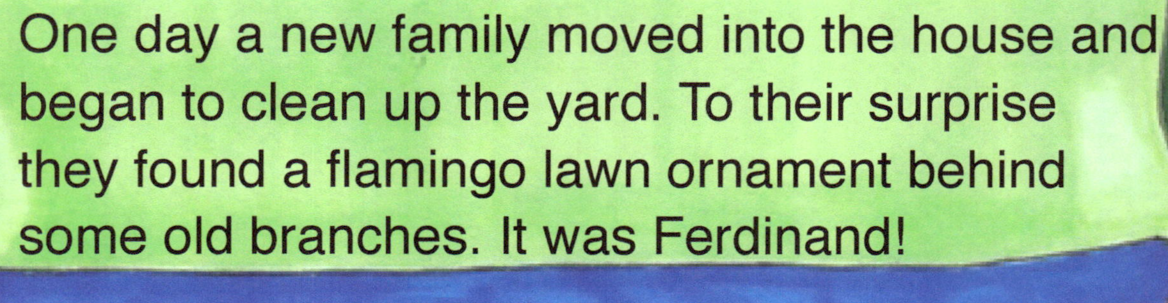

One day a new family moved into the house and began to clean up the yard. To their surprise they found a flamingo lawn ornament behind some old branches. It was Ferdinand!

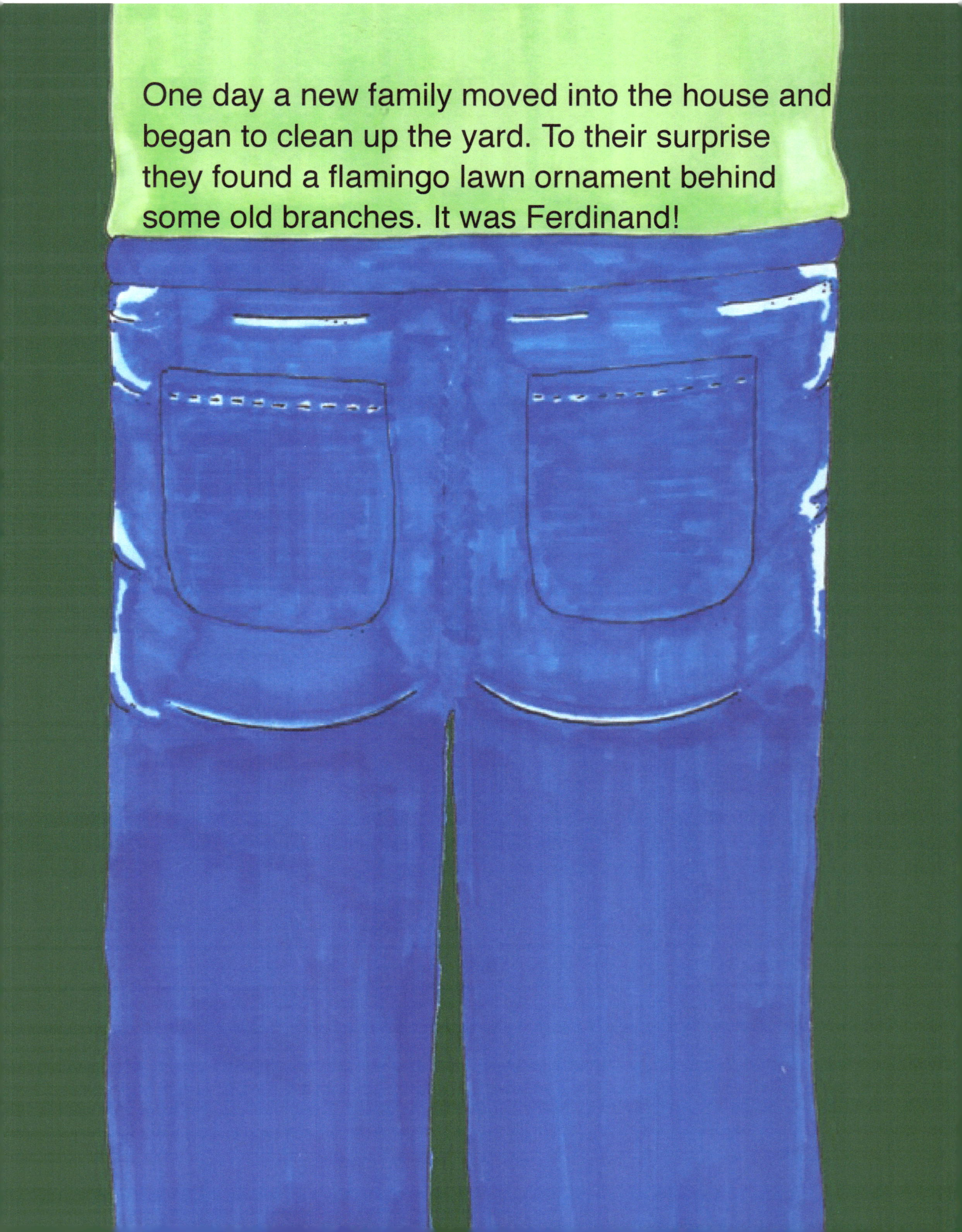

The family loved Ferdinand. They cleaned him up and gave him a new bow tie. They put him in a prominent spot in the yard right near the bird bath. Ferdinand was so happy to be seen. He could not wait until he could meet some new friends in the morning.

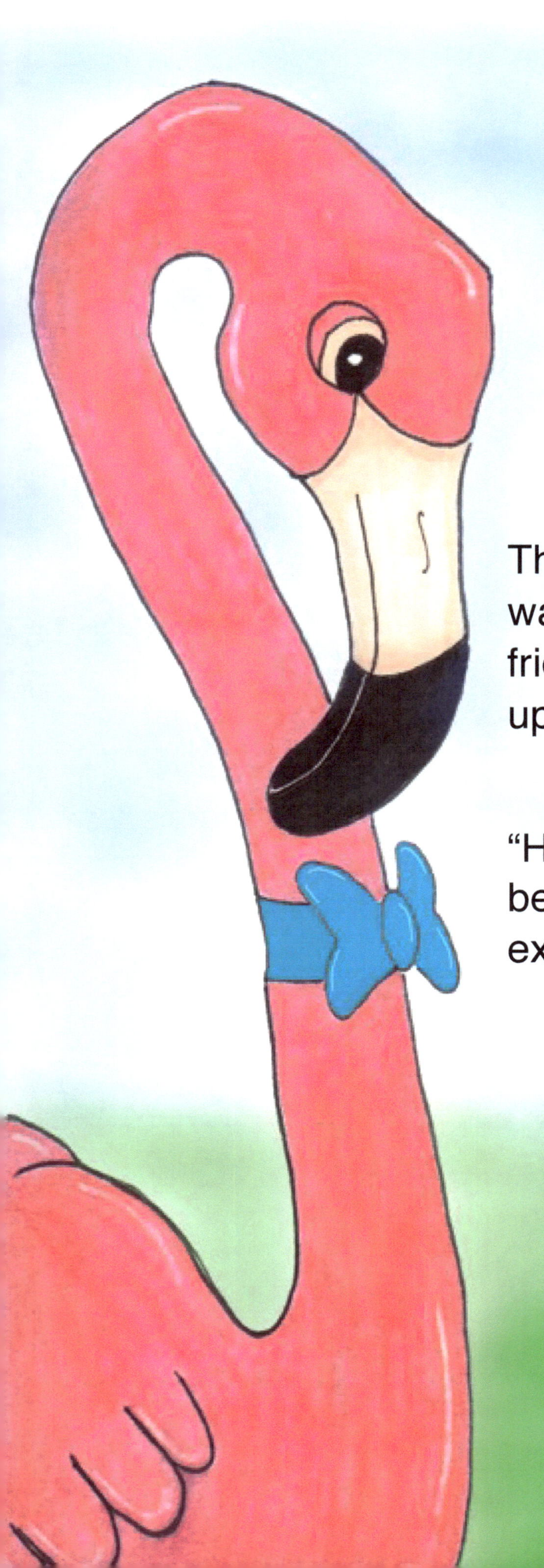

The next morning Ferdinand was ready to meet his new friends. Greta Goose waddled up to the yard first.

"Hi! I am Ferdinand. Can we be friends?" Ferdinand said excitedly.

The goose looked at Ferdinand. "I don't know," honked Greta Goose. "You are very different and have such a funny neck." And Greta waddled away.

Ferdinand was sad but he saw a woodpecker perched on a nearby tree.

Ferdinand got his courage up and spoke to the woodpecker. "Hi, I am Ferdinand. Can we be friends?"

Wilford the Woodpecker laughed and said, "I don't know. You are such a bright pink." Then he flew away still laughing.

Ferdinand felt very sad. He was so excited to meet new friends and it was not working out. A glint of hope filled Ferdinand as he saw a squirrel scurrying across the yard.

One more time Ferdinand introduced himself, "Hi I am Ferdinand. Can we be friends?"

The squirrel looked at Ferdinand and squeaked, "I don't know. You are a funny kind of bird. You don't even have real feathers." And Sarah the Squirrel scampered off into the trees.

Ferdinand cried. He always wanted to have great friends and belong but he still had none. As he cried, a cardinal landed on the bird bath.

"Don't cry. Nothing can be that bad. I am Cory the Cardinal. Is there anything I can do for you?" chirped Cory.

"I have no friends. All of the animals do not like me", sobbed Ferdinand.

Cory looked at Ferdinand and told him, "I will be your friend. Ferdinand you are like no other bird I have ever met." This was true. Although Ferdinand was unique, he also had many qualities like some of Cory's other friends. Cory had an idea and Ferdinand was happy that Cory was his new friend.

Ferdinand stood in the darkness under the full moon all night long and thought about what his new friend Cory said.

Ferdinand was happy Cory liked him just the way he was. Ferdinand thought with a friend like Cory anything was possible. Tomorrow would be a new day to make more friends.

Before the woodland animals made it to the yard
with Ferdinand, Cory stopped each of them to talk.

First he spoke to Greta. "Greta, why don't you like
my new friend, Ferdinand?" asked Cory.

Greta honked, "Well, he has such a long neck!"

Cory looked up at Greta and said, "Greta, I think his neck is beautiful and long like yours."

Greta thought about what Cory said and waddled on.

Next Cory saw Wilford and asked, "Why don't you like my new friend, Ferdinand?"

Wilford laughed, "Well, he is such a bright color!"

Cory replied, "I think his bright colors remind me
how you and I have such lovely bright red feathers."

Wilford thought about what Cory said and flew off.

Cory spotted Sarah scampering through the forest and asked, "Sarah, why don't you like my new friend Ferdinand?"

Sarah replied, "Well, he does not have real feathers!"

Cory thought about what she said and replied, "Sarah you do not have real feathers like me but instead have such beautiful soft fur."

Sarah blushed a little and thought about what Cory said as she scampered off.

All of the animals gathered in Ferdinand's yard. Cory greeted Ferdinand and stood right by his side when Greta Goose, Wilford Woodpecker, and Sarah Squirrel approached Ferdinand.

The animals were ashamed of how they had treated Ferdinand the day before. Ferdinand felt strong because he had his new friend Cory by his side.

"I am so sorry Ferdinand for my rudeness. I hope you can forgive me and we can be friends," honked Greta Goose.

"I am so sorry for laughing at you Ferdinand. I hope you can forgive me and we can be friends," chirped Wilford Woodpecker.

"Ferdinand, I am embarrassed for my behavior. We all want you to be our friend. Can you forgive us?" asked Sarah humbly.

Ferdinand looked at them all. He was filled with great joy that they could see him for who he was. "Yes, I forgive you all and would love to be your friend!" exclaimed Ferdinand.

This is the story of how I found my first friends. My friend, Cory, really made a difference in helping others understand that although we are different we are also the same. I am so happy to have new friends. I wonder who I will meet next. Who will be your next friend?

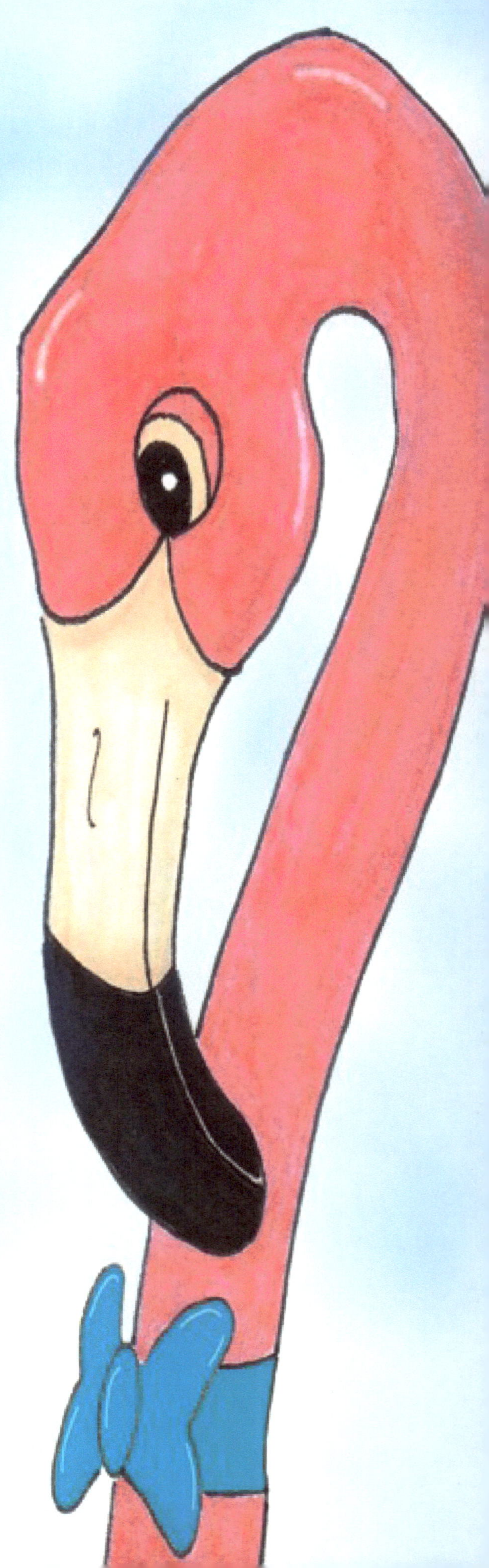